Please help the b[...]
Moonglow M[...]

Our brave and loyal friend, Arrow, has travelled far from our world to protect the magic key that keeps our kingdom safe from the dark rabbits. Arrow is very far from home and will need your help.

Could you be his friend?

This magic bunny might be hard to spot as he is very small and often appears in different fluffy bunny disguises – but you can recognize him by the rainbow twinkle in his eyes.

Thank you for your help!

Strike
Leader of Moonglow Meadow

Sue Bentley's books for children often include animals, fairies and magic. She lives in Northampton in a house surrounded by a hedge so she can pretend she's in the middle of the countryside. She loves reading and going to the cinema, and writes while watching the birds on the feeders outside her window and eating chocolate. Sue was brought up surrounded by small animals and loved them all — especially her gentle pet rabbits whose fur smelled so sweetly of rain and grass.

Sue Bentley

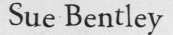

Chocolate Wishes

Illustrated by Angela Swan

PUFFIN

For Roger – so sleek and beautiful with coal-black fur

PUFFIN BOOKS

Published by the Penguin Group
Penguin Books Ltd, 80 Strand, London WC2R 0RL, England
Penguin Group (USA) Inc., 375 Hudson Street, New York, New York 10014, USA
Penguin Group (Canada), 90 Eglinton Avenue East, Suite 700, Toronto, Ontario, Canada M4P 2Y3
(a division of Pearson Penguin Canada Inc.)
Penguin Ireland, 25 St Stephen's Green, Dublin 2, Ireland (a division of Penguin Books Ltd)
Penguin Group (Australia), 250 Camberwell Road, Camberwell, Victoria 3124, Australia
(a division of Pearson Australia Group Pty Ltd)
Penguin Books India Pvt Ltd, 11 Community Centre, Panchsheel Park, New Delhi – 110 017, India
Penguin Group (NZ), 67 Apollo Drive, Rosedale, North Shore 0632, New Zealand
(a division of Pearson New Zealand Ltd)
Penguin Books (South Africa) (Pty) Ltd, 24 Sturdee Avenue, Rosebank,
Johannesburg 2196, South Africa

Penguin Books Ltd, Registered Offices: 80 Strand, London WC2R 0RL, England

puffinbooks.com

First published 2010
3

Text copyright © Sue Bentley, 2010
Illustrations copyright © Angela Swan, 2010
All rights reserved

The moral right of the author and illustrator has been asserted

Set in Bembo
Made and printed in England by Clays Ltd, St Ives plc

British Library Cataloguing in Publication Data
A CIP catalogue record for this book is available from the British Library

ISBN: 978–0–141–33241–3

www.greenpenguin.co.uk

Mixed Sources
Product group from well-managed
forests and other controlled sources
www.fsc.org Cert no. SA-COC-1592
© 1996 Forest Stewardship Council

Penguin Books is committed to a sustainable future
for our business, our readers and our planet.
The book in your hands is made from paper
certified by the Forest Stewardship Council.

Prologue

Arrow glanced around Moonglow
Meadow as he emerged from the
burrow. A rainbow shone in his warm
brown eyes. Lush grass waved gently in
the night breeze and the air was soft with
the scent of wild flowers. Other magic
rabbits were nibbling juicy leaves or
hopping about in the moonlight.

Bending his head, Arrow began

grooming his velvety white fur, which was flecked with silver. A tiny gold key he wore on a fine chain round his neck gave a bell-like tinkle. As the chosen keeper of the magical key, Arrow was responsible for looking after it.

A large older rabbit with a wise expression and a dark grey muzzle bounded towards him. Arrow saw that Strike looked tired and that there was dust in his fur.

'I did not expect you to return so soon.' Arrow bowed in greeting before the leader of the warren. 'When are the dark rabbits coming to live with us?'

Strike shook his head wearily. 'They refused. The dark rabbits are unwilling to share our land.'

'I do not understand.' Arrow was

puzzled. The deep gulley next to
Moonglow Meadow was home to a
neighbouring warren of dark rabbits.
Their land had become so dry that
nothing grew there any more and they
were hungry. 'How will they survive
without our help?'

'By stealing what we treasure the most!
Our magic key!' Strike rumbled, his face
darkening. 'They want to use it to make
their gulley green and beautiful again.
They are coming soon and are not far
behind me.'

Arrow gasped and his tail twitched
nervously. 'But without the key's power,
Moonglow Meadow will become a desert
and we will starve. What can we do?'

Strike extended a muscular paw and
rested it gently on Arrow's shoulder. 'You

must go to the Otherworld. Hide there with the key so the dark rabbits cannot find it.'

Arrow gulped at the thought of all the unknown dangers. He felt very young and afraid, but he took a deep breath and then lifted his head. 'I will do it.'

Strike smiled with pride and affection. 'There is no time to waste!' Lifting his head, he gave a soft but piercing cry.

Every rabbit in the warren pricked up its ears and came hurrying towards them. They formed a circle around Arrow. Suddenly, the golden key glowed so brightly that Arrow couldn't see a thing.

The light faded slowly and where the young white-and-silver magic rabbit had been now stood a tiny fluffy white bunny with huge golden-brown eyes that gleamed with tiny rainbows.

'Use this disguise,' Strike ordered. 'Only return when we need more of the key's magic to protect our meadow. And watch out for the black rabbits! They will be looking for you.'

Arrow straightened his small fluffy shoulders. 'I will not fail the warren!'

Thud. Thud. Thud. The rabbits began thumping their feet in time. Arrow felt the magic building and a cloud of crystal dust sparkled around him as Moonglow Meadow began to fade . . .

Chapter
ONE

Dawn Kenton's heart beat quickly as she opened the classroom door. She hoped her new teacher would find her someone friendly to sit next to. She was already missing her friends from her old school.

The teacher was taking the register. Dawn hovered in the doorway, not sure whether she ought to knock politely or say something.

Oh, great. I'm late on my very first day at my new school, she thought. She felt herself blushing as the whole class turned to look at her.

Just as Dawn was gathering her courage to speak, Miss Walker lifted her head and spotted her. She had short brown hair and glasses, and had seemed really nice when Dawn came to see the school with her mum and dad a few weeks ago.

She came over. 'Hello there. Come on in.' She put an encouraging hand on Dawn's shoulder and drew her into the classroom. 'Listen up, class. This is Dawn Kenton; she's just moved into the area. I want you all to make her feel welcome.'

'Hi, Dawn,' called a loud chorus of voices.

Dawn managed a shy grin.

Miss Walker pointed towards the back
of the room. 'There's a spare place next
to Emma Packard. Emma will show you
around, but remember to come and see
me if you ever have any problems. OK?'

'Thanks.' Head down, Dawn scooted
towards the empty chair.

Behind her, the teacher finished taking the register.

Two girls nudged each other and giggled as Dawn drew level with them. 'Let's see what Emma does!' one of them whispered.

Dawn tried not to swing round and look at them but she wondered what they meant. She sat down next to her new classmate and slid her school bag under the desk.

Emma pulled a face at the two girls who had whispered. She had short hair, blue eyes and a pretty heart-shaped face. Turning back to Dawn, she shrugged. 'Take no notice of Alesha and Vicky. They're just jealous cos I get to make a new friend! You can put your stuff in this drawer,' she said helpfully.

'Um . . . thanks,' Dawn said gratefully, relieved that Emma seemed nice.

It wasn't just her old school friends that Dawn missed, she was still feeling strange after moving into the new flat. Pets weren't allowed in Redford Mansions, so Tansy, Dawn's beloved Jack Russell, had gone to live with her aunt. Dawn knew it would be ages before she stopped missing her little dog.

As she bent down and began fishing about in her bag, her light-brown shoulder-length hair swung forward. Dawn tucked a strand behind one ear and with her free hand pulled out a pile of books.

'Oh!' she gasped as the heavy books slid out of her grip and fell to the floor with a crash.

The kids sitting nearby almost jumped out of their skins.

'Sorry,' Dawn murmured. She dropped to her knees and scrabbled about, picking up the books.

Emma leaned over to help her, but Dawn was so flustered she didn't notice. She got up quickly and her head accidentally brushed against Emma's forehead.

'Ow!' Emma exclaimed loudly, clapping her hand over her eye. 'You clumsy great twerp! You nearly knocked my eyebrow off!'

'Oh, gosh! Sorry . . .' Dawn chewed at her lip. She didn't think it had been *that* bad, but Emma was making so much fuss that Dawn didn't dare say anything. 'Maybe you need first aid or something.

I'll go and tell Miss.'

As she stood up, Emma and the two girls in front burst into giggles.

Dawn looked blankly at them. Emma seemed to have recovered completely. What was going on?

'Got you!' Emma laughed, her eyes sparkling. 'That was *too* easy!'

Dawn smiled awkwardly, trying to see the funny side.

'Is something wrong, dear?' Miss Walker called out.

'Um, no. I . . . I . . . I'm fine,' Dawn stuttered, only just realizing that she was still standing up. As dozens of pairs of eyes turned to stare at her she felt herself going bright red and she wished the floor would open up and swallow her. To her horror, she felt her eyes prickling with tears as she quickly plonked herself down again.

'All right, class,' the teacher clapped her hands. 'Take out your workbooks please. With Easter approaching, we're studying different customs round the world.'

'Hey, what's wrong?' Emma said, glancing sideways at Dawn.

Dawn blinked hard. She hated being made fun of and all of a sudden she missed her old life, her friends and Tansy even more. But she didn't say any of that.

'I'm fine,' she murmured again. 'Just leave me alone.'

Emma shrugged and bent over her workbook. 'Suit yourself.'

At lunchtime, Dawn found an empty table and sat by herself to eat her sandwiches. Emma was with a group of girls nearby. 'Hey, Dawn! Come over here!' she called.

Dawn thought about going over, but they were all laughing loudly and messing about. She didn't want to be the butt of their jokes for a second time that day, so she hunched her shoulders and pretended she hadn't heard.

The rest of the day seemed to crawl by. When the bell for home finally sounded, Dawn escaped as quickly as she could.

She grabbed her coat from the cloakroom and flew out of the school gate.

She swung her school bag by its long strap as she hurried home to the nearby flat. She sighed heavily, thinking about how before Tansy would have run to her the moment she got in, her stubby tail twirling. School and home really weren't very happy places to be right now.

Dawn turned into the neat gardens that surrounded Redford Mansions. It seemed quiet in there and she could sit by herself until she felt less upset. Otherwise her mum would notice that she looked glum and start asking questions, and she didn't want to worry her.

She threw her bag on a bench and sat down next to it. Suddenly, there was a bright flash, and a shower of crystal dust

drifted towards Dawn like a glimmering
cloud.

Dawn screwed up her face, trying to
make sense of what she was seeing. As the
dust slowly dissolved, she spotted a tiny
fluffy white bunny on the grass.

'Can you help me please?' it asked in a
scared little voice.

Chapter
TWO

Dawn's eyes widened as she stared
at the cute little bunny in complete
astonishment before shaking her head for
being silly. Talking animals only existed in
fairy tales, not in real life!

The bunny's long floppy ears lifted and
it twitched its pink nose nervously. Dawn
walked slowly forward and then hunched
down so she wouldn't frighten it.

'Hello there,' she said gently, reaching
out her hand. 'Aren't you gorgeous? I
wonder how you got here. You can't
belong to anyone in the flats.'

'That is true. I do not belong to
anyone. I have just arrived,' the bunny said
in a shaky little voice.

Dawn did a double take and only just
stopped herself jerking her hand back as if

she'd been burned. 'You . . . You really can talk! How come?'

'All of the rabbits in my world can talk,' Arrow told her, lifting his little head proudly. 'I am Arrow, guardian of Moonglow Meadow. May I know your name?'

'Um . . . yeah. I'm Dawn. Dawn Kenton. I live in one of these flats with my parents.' For the first time she noticed that the bunny had gorgeous melting brown eyes that seemed to glimmer with tiny rainbows.

Arrow bowed his head. 'I am honoured to meet you, Dawn.'

'Likewise.' Dawn bowed awkwardly. 'Where is Moonglow Meadow?' It sounded beautiful, but Dawn had never heard of such a place.

Arrow shook his head and something round his neck tinkled softly. Dawn saw that he wore a fine gold chain with a key hanging from it. 'Moonglow Meadow is where my warren lives.'

Dawn nodded. She knew that 'warren' was the name used for a group of rabbits who all lived together. At her old school she'd done a project about animal groups. 'I didn't know there were any meadows or fields near here. Is it far away?'

'Yes, very far. In another world,' Arrow explained. 'I am keeper of the magic key, which keeps our meadow lush and green. But our neighbours, who are fierce dark rabbits, are trying to steal it. Their land is dry and stony, and they will not share the meadow with us. They want to use the key's magic to change their own land.

If they do this, Moonglow Meadow will become a desert.'

'Oh no! That would be awful!' Dawn exclaimed.

'Yes, it would. That is why I was sent here to hide and keep the magic key safe.'

Dawn nodded slowly, looking at the tiny bunny more closely. 'I don't mean to be rude, but aren't you a bit small for such an important mission?'

Rainbows gleamed more brightly in Arrow's warm brown eyes. 'Please stand clear,' he ordered, rising up on to his back legs.

Dawn felt a strange warm prickling sensation down her spine as the key round his neck began flashing and a cloud of shimmering crystal dust swirled about Arrow. When it cleared, Dawn saw that

the cute little bunny had vanished and
in his place stood the most amazing and
majestic rabbit she had ever seen. It was
as big as a large cat and had silky white
fur flecked with silver. The tips of its
ears looked as if they'd been dipped in
silver glitter and its chocolate-brown eyes
flashed with jewel-bright rainbows.

Dawn gasped. Nothing could have prepared her for such a magnificent sight.

'Arrow?' she gulped in wonderment.

'Yes, it is still me, Dawn,' Arrow said in a smooth velvety voice.

Before she had got used to seeing Arrow in his true form there was a final glow of light from his key and he appeared as a tiny fluffy white bunny again.

'Wow! That's an amazing disguise!'

Arrow twitched his white whiskers nervously. 'I am afraid it will not fool the dark rabbits if any of them find me. I must hide quickly.'

'You can stay with m–' Dawn began eagerly. 'Oh, I keep forgetting that we're not allowed pets in our new flat.'

Arrow dipped his head in a shallow

bow. 'I understand. I will ask another person to help me. Thank you for your kindness. It was nice to meet you, Dawn.' He took two small hops towards a nearby bush.

'No! Please, wait!' Dawn burst out.

She couldn't bear to lose him, especially as no one else had been friendly to her all day. As a big strong rabbit with thick white fur Arrow was magnificent as guardian of his meadow. But as a tiny fluffy bunny with melting brown eyes he was totally adorable and Dawn just wanted to help him.

She thought hard. 'I know! I'll smuggle you into our flat inside my school bag. Mum's going shopping straight after work and Dad's not back for ages, so no one will notice. You can live in my bedroom with me.'

Arrow's eyes twinkled gratefully.
'Thank you, Dawn. I would like to live
with you very much.'

Dawn opened her school bag and
placed it on the ground. Arrow kicked
up his back legs, leapt inside and settled
down next to her tiger-print pencil case.

'Let's go!' Dawn zipped the bag, leaving a small opening so he could breathe. They went into Redford Mansions through the main doors. 'We're on the third floor, so I usually use the lift. It might feel a bit odd to you at first,' she warned him.

'I am not afraid. I know that I will be safe with you,' Arrow said in a muffled voice.

Dawn felt a surge of pride that the tiny little bunny trusted her. She was looking forward to taking care of Arrow and finding out more about him. It might even help her feel a bit less lonely for Tansy. Her heart felt lighter than it had for days.

Chapter
THREE

'There. How's that?' Dawn tucked Arrow
into the cosy nest she'd just made by
tucking a woollen scarf inside an old
shoebox.

Arrow snuffled about, nibbling and
pawing at the scarf before curling up with
his nose between his fluffy white paws.
'This is a good place to sleep.'

Dawn smiled, delighted that he liked

it. She picked up the box, ready to take it into her bedroom, when the kitchen door banged open. Her mum staggered in with two shopping bags.

Dawn jumped guiltily. She had no chance to hide Arrow. 'Mum! You're back!'

'Hi, love!' Mrs Kenton said cheerily. Crossing the room, she dumped the shopping on the work surface. 'I was quicker than I expected. They opened a new till just as I got to the check-out.'

She started unpacking groceries. 'How
was your first day at school?'

Dawn braced herself for a serious
telling-off when her mum eventually
spotted Arrow in the kitchen. From the
corner of her eye she noticed that the key
round Arrow's neck was glowing again. 'It
was . . . erm, OK,' she said vaguely.

Why hadn't Mum said anything about
Arrow? It was almost as if she hadn't
seen him.

'What's that you're clutching?' Mrs
Kenton nodded towards the shoebox as
she put a carton of milk in the fridge.
'Is it part of a class project?'

'Yeah! We're doing . . .' Dawn fought
for an explanation '. . . Easter stuff. I'm
going to work on it in my bedroom. See
you later!' She shot out of the kitchen

and hurried into her bedroom.

Once the door was closed, Dawn placed Arrow's box on her bedside chest of drawers. 'Phew! That was close. I thought I was toast back there. Why didn't Mum see you?'

Arrow's tail waggled cheekily. 'I used my magic to make myself invisible. Now only you will be able to see me and hear me talking to you.'

'Fine by me! It makes it easier to hide you from Mum and Dad. Is anyone else allowed to know?'

'No. My presence here must be kept secret,' Arrow said, looking serious. 'You can tell no one about me, Dawn.'

Dawn felt disappointed. She had wondered if Emma would be nicer to her if she knew a magic bunny had chosen her for his friend. But she was prepared to keep Arrow's secret, if it would help keep him and his key safe from the fierce dark rabbits. She didn't want to lose her only friend here.

'OK, then. Cross my heart,' she promised.

'Thank you, Dawn.'

Dawn stroked his velvety ears with the tips of her fingers. 'Why does that key round your neck keep flashing?'

'It makes my magic stronger,' he explained. 'When its power is needed for Moonglow Meadow the key will glow continuously. And I will have to return.' As he finished speaking, Arrow's whiskers quivered and he yawned sleepily.

Dawn would have liked to ask him more about his strange and wonderful world, but he had already closed his eyes

with a sigh. Almost at once soft little
bunny snores rose from the box.

Dawn gently tucked the scarf around
her fluffy new friend. She'd only known
Arrow for a short time but she already
loved him to bits.

Dawn heard her dad come home from
work and so she left Arrow snoozing
while she went in to eat supper with her
mum and dad. Later, she was helping to
clear away the plates when the phone

went in the hall.

Dawn dashed to answer it. It was Aunt Jenny, her mum's sister.

'Hello, Aunt Jenny! How's Tansy? Is she missing me? Have you taken her for lots of walks?' The pent-up questions spilled out of her. 'She loves it in the park. Her favourite food is meaty chunks. And how's she getting on with Bella? Have they been playing together?' Bella was her aunt's gentle old Labrador.

'Whoa! Slow down, love!' Dawn could tell her aunt was smiling. 'Tansy's doing fine, although she's running rings round poor old Bella. We're giving her lots of extra cuddles. Don't worry about her,' she said in her kind sensible way.

'I'm trying not to, but I miss her loads,' Dawn said sadly. She knew that she always would, but she had to try to be grown-up about this. Tansy had a good home with her aunt and Bella for company. 'Can I come and see her this weekend?'

'Come any time you like. It's always lovely to see you,' Aunt Jenny said warmly. 'Tansy's still your dog, you know. She always will be.' After they'd chatted for a few more minutes, they said their goodbyes and Dawn passed the phone to her mum.

Dawn had a lump in her throat. She swallowed hard, determined not to cry as she left her mum and aunt chatting and wandered into the kitchen. Putting thoughts of Tansy aside, she opened the fridge and chose a carrot and some juicy lettuce leaves.

Stuffing the food under her top, Dawn

went into her bedroom to see if Arrow was awake. The box on her bedside chest was empty.

'Arrow?' she whispered, looking around.

There was a faint scrabbling noise. A pink nose followed by a fluffy little head with pricked ears appeared from beneath the bed. 'I have been exploring your territory,' Arrow said, his nose twitching.

Dawn smiled. She'd never thought of her bedroom as 'territory' before – but she supposed it was in a way! She sank down on to the bedside mat beside him and pulled out the food.

'Are you hungry? I don't know what magic bunnies eat, so I got you these.'

'In Moonglow Meadow I eat juicy grass and sweet wild flowers. This is strange food!' Arrow hopped forward and

nudged the carrot, sniffing it curiously.
He took a tiny nibble and then did the
same with a lettuce leaf. 'I like it!'

Dawn watched, smiling as he munched
through the food and then groomed
himself. When he'd finished, she lifted
Arrow on to her bed and lay down with
him sprawled out full length on her chest.

She cuddled his warm little body
delightedly, enjoying the clean grassy
scent of his fur. 'I can't wait for you to

meet Tansy. I'm going to see her this
weekend. She belongs to me, but she's
gone to live with my Aunt Jenny and
Bella,' she explained.

'I would like to meet Tansy very much.
What sort of rabbit is she?' Arrow asked,
tucking his front paws beneath him.

Dawn laughed. 'Tansy isn't a rabbit!
She's a white-and-brown Jack Russell
terrier.'

'A dog?' Arrow blinked at her
nervously. 'I know of these, but we do not
have any in Moonglow Meadow. Is Tansy
friendly?'

'Oh yes. She wouldn't hurt a fly,'
Dawn assured him confidently, although
she wasn't actually sure that her little
dog had ever met a rabbit before. She
was looking forward to all the fun Tansy

and Arrow would have, playing chase
around her aunt's huge garden.

Chapter
FOUR

The following morning Dawn woke to
find something furry curled up right
under her chin. It took a moment for her
to realize that it was Arrow and he was
trembling all over.

'Hey, what's wrong?' she whispered,
stroking him gently.

The magic bunny sat up, blinking his
big brown eyes. 'I thought one of those

giant noisy monsters that grumble outside was chasing me!'

Dawn frowned, listening hard, but there were only a few cars going past the flat. That's what he meant! So many things in this big new world must seem strange and scary to the tiny bunny.

'Cars and buses aren't monsters. They're just things people travel about in. I used to be a bit scared of them when I was little. Don't worry, I won't let them hurt you. I'm very good at crossing roads,' she reassured him.

Arrow had stopped trembling. 'I must try to be braver,' he decided.

'I think you're already a brave little bunny!' Dawn crooned. 'It took heaps of courage to come here on this mission.'

'Thank you, Dawn.' He touched her

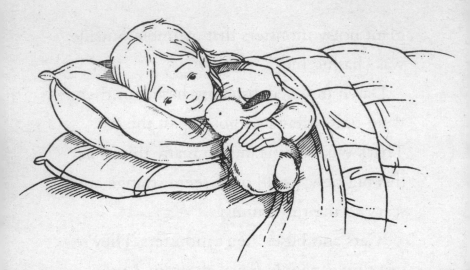

chin with the tip of his damp pink nose.

'You're welcome! I love having you
for my friend. I really wish we could
spend all day together.' She pulled a face.
'Unfortunately, I have to get ready for
school instead. It's my second day in my
new class.'

'What is school?'

'It's where kids go to learn things,'
Dawn explained.

Arrow's cute face lit up with eagerness. 'We do not have such things in Moonglow Meadow. I will come with you!'

'I don't know if that's a good idea,' Dawn said doubtfully, imagining the complications of having a bunny hopping around the classroom – even an invisible one. But then her tummy fluttered at the thought of being teased or laughed at again and she decided it would be good to have her magical new friend with her.

'Well, all right then,' she agreed.

After a quick breakfast, Dawn and Arrow hurried to school. They made it to the playground as the bell was sounding for lessons. Dawn filed inside to the cloakroom with everyone else.

Some kids she recognized from yesterday's class smiled at her. Dawn smiled back as she hung up her coat. She turned round, about to speak to them, but they were already walking away, chattering excitedly about the Easter celebrations. Everyone was so distracted with Easter that Dawn thought she would never make friends!

Her smile faded as she unzipped her bag. She was really glad that Arrow was here.

The magic bunny had just popped his head out of the opening when a hand snatched her bag and whisked it away.

Arrow gave a startled cry.

'Hey! Don't! You'll hurt him!' Dawn cried without thinking. Whipping round, she saw Emma clutching the bag to her chest.

'Hurt who?' Emma asked. 'Have you
brought your ickle teddy bear to school
wiv oo den?' she joked in a silly baby
voice.

Dawn was too worried about Arrow to
care what Emma thought. 'Give me my

bag! Now!' she demanded.

'Why don't I see what's in it first?'
Emma teased, her eyes sparkling. 'Do
you have something yummy in your
lunchbox? I've got some of Mum's
lemon cake. Tell you what! I'll swap
you some.'

Dawn hesitated, puzzled. Emma almost
seemed to be making some kind of effort
now, but she was too terrified that Arrow
was going to get squashed to think any
more of it. She lunged forward and tried
to grab her bag back.

Emma danced away, holding it up out
of reach. Dawn stood still, feeling helpless.
She knew this game. It could go on
for ages.

Suddenly, she felt a warm prickling
sensation down her spine. Something very

strange was about to happen.

Dawn saw a puff of crystal dust shoot up out of the bag's opening. The dust transformed into a big whoosh of what looked like thin brightly coloured tentacles.

Pink, yellow and blue, they made comical whizzing and burping noises as they shot out in all directions, forming a ragged clump and making a beeline for Emma.

Splat! Splop! Sploosh!

Emma's head, shoulders and the front of her school uniform were immediately covered in sticky party streamers.

'Aargh! Get it off me!' she cried in a panic, throwing up her arms in shock. Dawn's bag went sailing high up into the air.

'Arrow!' Dawn almost tripped over her

own feet as she tried to catch it.

Her fingers closed on thin air as the bag hovered out of reach for a moment and then floated away to land gently on a bench at the far side of the cloakroom. Arrow hopped out with a flick of his fluffy tail and sat there looking innocent with rainbows dancing in his big brown eyes. He waved a front paw at Dawn to show he was fine.

'Phew!' Dawn's heartbeat slowly returned to normal.

Luckily, Emma hadn't noticed the floating bag. 'Yuck! This stuff's gross!' she complained, going cross-eyed as she pulled bits of twirly pink stuff off the end of her nose.

Dawn felt laughter bubbling up in her. 'I thought you liked jokes!' she spluttered.

Emma didn't answer. She shook herself
like a wet dog and the streamers tumbled
on to the floor and started to dissolve.

Dawn went over to Arrow. She picked
him up, tucked him under one arm and
grabbed her bag, before heading towards
the door to the classroom. 'Arrow! That
was so naughty!' she scolded gently. 'But
maybe Emma will stop being such a pain
with me now. Oops, sorry!' She only just

managed to stop herself from knocking
into Miss Walker, who was coming into
the cloakroom.

'Why aren't you two in class? What's
going on?' the teacher asked.

'I . . . erm . . .' Dawn didn't know quite
what to say without getting into trouble,
but she wasn't going to snitch.

But Miss Walker seemed to have
worked things out for herself. Frowning,
she turned to Emma. 'Look at you
covered in mess. I expect you've been
playing silly tricks again. I'm very
disappointed in you. I expected you to
make Dawn welcome and help her settle
down in class.'

'I was only messing about with her bag
as a joke!' Emma argued, looking at Dawn
with a wounded expression. 'It was meant

to be funny.'

'Jokes aren't funny if no one's laughing, Emma,' the teacher said firmly. 'Now I want you both in class. Pronto!'

Hanging her head, Emma went to the classroom. Dawn walked beside her, no longer feeling like laughing. Why did she have the feeling that this time what happened hadn't been all Emma's fault?

She sighed. It looked like being another long school day, sitting next to each other without speaking.

Chapter
FIVE

'I don't know what I'd do without you in class!' Dawn whispered to Arrow on Saturday morning. They were in the supermarket with her mum. 'Since Miss Walker told us about the Easter Fayre everyone's too busy to be friends. And Emma's always with Alesha and Vicky. She probably hates me after she got into trouble with Miss in the cloakroom.'

Arrow was sitting with his front legs
looped over the opening of her shoulder
bag. He looked up at her. 'Perhaps she
would like it if you talked to her. I do not
think that Emma is a mean person,' he
said wisely.

Dawn fell silent as she wondered
whether Arrow could be right. But even
if she wanted to make things up with

Emma, she didn't know how to start.

She soon forgot about Emma when she noticed Arrow licking his lips at a display of particularly juicy carrots. Reaching for a bag, she filled it right up. Mrs Kenton raised her eyebrows as Dawn dumped the carrots in the shopping trolley.

'Are you sure you're feeling all right?'

'Yep! I *love* carrots! But that doesn't mean I don't want any Easter eggs!' Dawn added hastily. She was a big fan of chocolate.

Her mum laughed. 'I think I'm finished. Let's go. You must be looking forward to seeing Tansy.' They were going to Aunt Jenny's house straight after the supermarket.

'You bet!' Dawn exclaimed. 'Can we pop into the pet shop on the way please?

I want to get a present for Tansy.' *And something for Arrow,* she thought.

Her mum nodded. 'No problem. I'll park outside and wait for you in the car.'

In the shop, Dawn counted out her spending money. There was just enough for a dog biscuit shaped like a bone and a rabbit chew made from parsley and wheat. Before going back to the car, Dawn hid the rabbit treat in her pocket so her mum wouldn't be suspicious.

A few minutes later, they drew up to her aunt's front drive and her mum climbed out. 'Here we are,' Dawn whispered excitedly to Arrow, who was standing on his back legs and peering out of the side window. 'I can't wait for you to meet Tansy.'

Her aunt appeared at the garden gate.

Bella, her elderly Labrador, was at her side and she had a little brown-and-white dog in her arms.

'Hi, Aunt Jenny! Bella! Tansy!' Dawn called, waving as she opened the car door. She glanced quickly over her shoulder at Arrow. 'I think you should jump into my bag for a start –' she began to say.

All of a sudden Tansy wriggled free from Aunt Jenny. Yapping excitedly, she exploded out of the front gate, bounded straight into the car and into Dawn's lap.

Arrow's muffled squeal of panic was lost in a torrent of barking and tail wagging. The magic bunny hastily leapt under the front seat.

'Hello, girl! Have you missed me then?' Dawn grabbed Tansy's collar as the little dog licked her chin and the end of her

nose. 'Hey! I've had a wash today! Calm
down. There's someone I want you to
meet!'

Tansy's nose twitched. She stiffened
as she seemed to catch Arrow's scent.
'Wroof!' An eager whine rumbled in her

throat as she struggled to get free again.

'Be gentle!' Dawn scolded, hanging on tight. 'It's OK, Arrow. Tansy's just excited. She won't hurt . . . Oh!'

'Grrr–uuf!' Tansy had slipped her collar. She peered down under the front seat, her mouth lolling open in a doggy grin as she prepared to jump at the magic bunny.

Arrow had other ideas. He shot out of the car and streaked round the side of the house. Tansy gave chase, barking with excitement.

'Oh my gosh!' Dawn almost fell on to the pavement as she scrambled after them.

Aunt Jenny and Mrs Kenton watched, open-mouthed, as Arrow, Tansy and then Dawn rushed past them.

'Wherever did that little white rabbit come from?' Aunt Jenny exclaimed.

Oh no! Dawn realized that Arrow
must have forgotten to stay invisible! She
pounded down the garden path, just in
time to see him leap into a bush at the
bottom.

Tansy wasn't far behind Arrow. She
skidded to a halt, tail wagging. With a
triumphant bark, she plunged in head first
after him.

Dawn saw something golden glow
in the depth of the bush. The magic
key! She felt the familiar warm tingling
sensation down her spine as a tall column
of shimmering crystal dust rose from
the bush. There was a rustle of frantic
movement, followed by a surprised bark.

'Yipe!' Tansy shot upwards out of the
bush like a cork from a bottle.

The little Jack Russell landed on top

of a very small birdhouse that was
hanging from a tree overhead. Tansy
perched there, balancing on the tips of all
four paws. Flattening her ears, she whined
nervously as she looked down at the lawn.

Dawn couldn't help smiling at her

mournful expression. 'I warned you about being too rough! Arrow's a very special little rabbit!'

Arrow hopped out from under the bush. He looked up at Tansy indignantly, dusting himself down with his fluffy front paws.

'I'm sorry, Arrow. I should have warned you that Tansy gets overexcited. Are you OK?'

The magic bunny nodded. 'I am fine now.'

'Good. So how about you two making friends?' she whispered as she heard her mum, her aunt and Bella approaching. 'Tansy needs to get down from there. And I think you need to become invisible.'

The key round Arrow's neck glowed brightly and a final cloud of sparkling

crystal dust surrounded Tansy, carrying
her gently down on to the lawn. Arrow
hopped up to the little dog, touched
his nose to hers and then sprang away.
Wagging her tail, Tansy padded carefully
after Arrow.

Dawn breathed. 'Phew! Panic over!'

'Where did that little white rabbit go?'
Dawn's mum asked, as she drew level.

'Um . . . it ran off. I think it was a wild
one . . .' Dawn replied.

Aunt Jenny nodded. 'That's probably it.
Look at Tansy, showing off in front you.
She was having a lovely game of chase all
by herself. It's a shame that Bella's too old
to run about with her.'

Dawn grinned as she watched Tansy
and Arrow playing their secret game. She
spent a happy hour playing with them

both before enjoying a delicious picnic
of sandwiches and yummy home-made
chocolate cake. Before leaving, Dawn
gave Tansy the bone-shaped biscuit.
She immediately settled down with
it between her front paws, gnawing it
happily.

Dawn tried not to feel too sad as they
headed back. Tansy was obviously well
cared for, but the visit had reminded her

how much she missed her little dog.

'I wish I could have brought her back with us,' she whispered to Arrow, who was nibbling his rabbit chew.

Her fluffy friend stopped munching long enough to rub his soft cheek against her hand. 'I hope that Tansy will be able to live with you again one day.'

'Me too,' Dawn sighed. At least she had Arrow as a friend. She felt herself cheering up as she stroked him.

Chapter
SIX

It was Friday, the day before the Easter
Fayre. In the school hall, kids were
busily pinning up a banner that read
'Pets' Corner: prizes for the best kept
pet'. Others were blowing up balloons,
organizing stalls with games and
arranging things for sale.

Dawn stood with a group of kids,
waiting to be given a job. She was

holding Arrow's invisible little body in
the crook of one arm, over which she'd
looped her school jumper.

Arrow craned his neck, watching all the
activity with interest. 'What is this for?'

'It's called Easter,' Dawn whispered
after quickly checking that no one was
watching her. 'People go to church
and have parties and eat lots of special
stuff like chocolate eggs and cupcakes
decorated with fluffy chicks and bunnies.
Not real ones,' she said, trying not to
smile as Arrow's eyes widened in alarm.

Nearby, Miss Walker was giving out

more jobs. The barrel needs to be filled with shredded paper for the Lucky Dip . . .'

Suddenly, there was a loud bang as a balloon burst.

Everyone laughed, but poor Arrow almost jumped out of his fur. His ears flattened in terror and he leapt to the floor. He darted behind a wooden stand that was leaning against a wall and crouched there trembling.

'. . . and if someone would like to put that notice stand together please,' Miss Walker was saying. 'It needs to go outside the door and –'

'I'll do it!' Dawn was across the room in a trice and bending down to scoop the scared little bunny into her arms. His tiny heart was fluttering against her hand.

'It's OK, Arrow,' she whispered. 'I know it was a very loud noise, but silly old bursting balloons can't hurt you.'

'I will not be frightened by such loud noises again,' Arrow announced proudly.

'Good for you.' Dawn tried not to smile too much. She had her back to everyone, so risked a hasty cuddle as she carried him to a nearby bookcase and put him gently on the top. 'There you go. No one will tread on you now.'

Arrow's eyes lit up as he spotted a spider plant and immediately began nibbling one of the leaves.

'Hey, leave that alone!' Dawn said. It could be very awkward to explain what was happening if someone noticed the plant's leaves gradually disappearing.

'Charming!' said a familiar voice.

Dawn whipped round in surprise, realizing that she'd spoken more loudly than she'd intended to. Emma was there and had obviously assumed Dawn was talking to her.

'I only came over to help you with that wooden sign thing,' Emma said huffily.

'I wasn't talking to . . . I didn't mean . . .' Dawn spread her hands helplessly as she knew she couldn't explain about Arrow.

'Don't bother!' Emma stormed off to help with the Lucky Dip.

Dawn watched her go in disbelief. After this, Emma would never want to be friends with her.

After breakfast on Saturday morning, Dawn phoned her aunt to see how Tansy was getting on. Her aunt held the phone close to Tansy, so the little dog could hear Dawn's voice. 'Be good for Aunt Jenny, Tansy! Love you lots.' Dawn made kissing noises down the phone and felt the usual tug of sadness as she heard Tansy's soft little whine. She could hardly bear to wait another week until she saw her again.

'Everything OK, love?' her dad asked, squeezing Dawn's shoulder gently as she rang off.

Dawn nodded.

'You need cheering up. Come on. Let's go to the Easter Fayre. I'm looking forward to seeing your classroom and meeting some of your new friends.' He jingled the car keys as he went towards the open front door. 'Your mum's already in the car.'

'I'll be right there!' Dawn raced to her room to fetch Arrow, who was just finishing his breakfast carrot.

At the school they joined the other kids and their parents filing into the classrooms for the Easter Fayre. The hall was bustling with people enjoying themselves. Older children from the school music club were on the stage playing their instruments. Dawn grinned as two little girls from the Reception class

71

pulled cheeky faces at her. Their faces were painted to look like cute Easter bunnies and they wore headbands with long pink ears!

Miss Walker came over to greet them. 'Hi, Dawn. Hello, Mr and Mrs Kenton. Glad you could make it.'

'Hi, Miss Walker,' Dawn said. 'It looks great in here.'

'Yes, it does. Everyone's worked really hard to get things ready. Including Dawn,' she said warmly. 'Dawn, would you like to sell some raffle tickets while I have a quick word with your mum and dad?'

Dawn took a bundle of tickets and she and Arrow set off round the hall.

Dawn wandered about, selling tickets as she went. Inside her shoulder bag, Arrow stretched up on his haunches so he could

look out. His little pink nose twitched at
all the exciting smells.

Over at Pets' Corner, Emma was
holding a large glossy black rabbit in
her arms. The judge presented her with
a shiny gold rosette. 'First prize goes
to Emma Packard's beautiful rabbit
Blackberry!'

'Yay!' Emma kissed her rabbit's head. 'We won! Well done, Blackberry.'

Arrow spotted the big black rabbit and Dawn felt him stiffen inside her bag. 'My enemies have found me!'

'What? Where?' Dawn spun round and clutched her bag protectively. 'Oh, you mean Emma's rabbit. That's not –'

She was too late. In a single mighty leap, Arrow landed on the floor and dashed under the nearest table.

'Oh no!' Dawn shot into action. Hastily thrusting a handful of coins and raffle tickets into her jeans pocket, she threw herself to her knees and scuttled under the table after her friend. 'Arrow, wait!'

Arrow took no notice. In his desperation to escape his fierce enemies he raced about blindly. Dawn lost sight of him and crawled out from under a table to look around the hall.

There he was! Somehow he'd ended up right back near Emma, who had just put Blackberry back into his carrier. Dawn saw Emma's eyes widen as she spotted the terrified little bunny. Bending down, she picked him up.

With a sinking heart, Dawn realized that Arrow was so scared that he'd forgotten to stay invisible again – just like when Tansy had chased him!

'Hello. Aren't you gorgeous? I'm sure no one brought a little white bunny here today. You must be lost.' Emma was cradling Arrow gently in her arms. 'Do you want to come home with me? You can be a friend for Blackberry.'

Dawn froze. *Now* what was she going to do?

Chapter
SEVEN

Dawn spoke without thinking. 'That
bunny's mine!' she blurted out as she
raced towards Emma.

'Excuse me? I don't think so. Where's
its carrier then? Anyway, I saw it first and
I'm keeping it.' Emma held Arrow gently
but firmly, a determined look on her face.

'Arrow's a him. Just give him to me,
Emma!'

Dawn bit her lip. She knew Arrow
couldn't use his magic to save himself
with so many people around. It was up
to her to sort this out somehow.

A few kids had wandered over to
admire the fluffy white bunny. Other
heads were turning to look at them.

Dawn tried to calm down and reason
with Emma. 'Look, I can't explain. But it's

really important that you give him to me,'
she said desperately.

Emma frowned. 'Why? Oh, I get it. You
think I won't look after him properly!'

'No. Of course you would. Blackberry's
gorgeous. It's not that . . .' Dawn's mind
seemed to have gone blank. How could
she explain without giving away Arrow's
secret? To make things worse, she saw
her parents coming over. *Oh, great*, she
groaned inwardly.

'Dawn? What's going on?' her mum
asked.

Dawn took a deep breath. 'It's this cute
little white rabbit. He needs a home.'

Her mum looked closely at Arrow.
'How odd. It looks just like the one Tansy
was chasing the other day at Aunt Jenny's.'

Dawn shook her head firmly. 'No. That

was definitely a wild one, remember? So can I have him? Please, Mum? Dad? He'd take up hardly any room. I'll do anything – washing-up, ironing. I'll even wash the car for a whole month and you needn't pay me . . .'

'Huh?' Emma frowned. 'I thought you said he was already yours?'

Dawn didn't answer. Luckily, no one was paying Emma any attention.

She crossed her finger and toes and screwed her eyes shut. Please, please let Mum and Dad say yes!

'I'm sorry, love,' her mum said gently. 'You know the rules about pets.'

'Your mum's right,' her dad said. 'But I know how much you miss Tansy. Maybe we could get you a goldfish.'

Dawn's spirits sank. She didn't want a

goldfish, she wanted Arrow back! There
was nothing she could do but watch
Emma open Blackberry's pet carrier, slip
Arrow inside and fasten the door.

Arrow seemed to have realized that
Blackberry wasn't one of the fierce black
rabbits from his homeland, but his brown
eyes still pleaded with Dawn through the
wire mesh side. 'Do I have to go home

with Emma? I want to stay with you.'

Dawn felt her heart turn over as she
bent close to whisper so that only he
could hear. 'I know. I want that too. Don't
worry! I'll think of some way of getting
you back. Promise.'

'Gotta go!' Emma sang out, picking up
the carrier. 'Mum and Dad are waiting for
me in the car park!' She stalked towards
the open door and went outside.

Dawn swallowed angry tears. Despite
her promise to Arrow, she didn't see how
she was going to get him back.

*There's no way I'm giving up! I have to do
something*, she told herself firmly.

As Dawn struggled to think of a plan,
something shiny on the hall floor caught
her eye.

Arrow's magic key!

It must have come off when Emma picked him up. Moonglow Meadow needed the key's magic to stay lush and green. She had to get it back to him!

Dawn raced outside. 'I'll be right back!' she called over her shoulder to her parents.

In her haste, Dawn slipped over on to the side of her foot and a hot pain shot through her ankle. Trying to ignore it, she frantically scanned the rows of parked cars. There! She spotted Emma putting the pet carrier in the back of a red car.

'Wait! I have to talk to you!' Dawn cried, half-running and half-limping over.

Emma straightened and looked at her in surprise.

Dawn saw that Emma's parents were talking to some people a few metres away. It was now or never. Inside the car, Arrow's little face was pressed hopefully against the wire mesh.

'Emma, please listen,' Dawn puffed. 'This is going to sound totally weird, but it's the truth. I swear.'

Emma folded her arms. 'Go on then.'

'I couldn't tell you this in there, but that little white bunny really is mine,' Dawn rushed on. 'I smuggled Arrow into my bedroom and he lives there. Mum and Dad would go ballistic if they knew. No pets are allowed in Redford Mansions . . .'

'Redford Mansions? Is that where you live?' Emma interrupted.

'Yes. We've just moved into one of the flats,' Dawn carried on, eager to get Arrow back. 'I brought Arrow here in my shoulder bag, but he got scared by something and jumped out. I was just about to put him back in my bag, when you picked him up.'

Emma blinked at her, obviously not sure whether to believe what she was saying. Then her lips curved in a smile. 'Wow! That's so cool. Fancy you doing that. I thought you were dead boring. You hardly say a word to anybody in class — especially me.'

'I can be a bit shy with new people and everybody's been so busy,' Dawn admitted, blushing. 'And . . . and I don't like being teased.'

'Yeah, well. I can be shy sometimes too.'

Dawn's jaw nearly dropped. Emma? Shy?

'People don't notice because I cover it up by making jokes and stuff. Maybe I go too far sometimes,' Emma admitted. 'I'm sorry.' Suddenly, she seemed to make up her mind. 'OK. You can have Arrow back, but you have to promise me something.'

Dawn frowned suspiciously. 'What?'

'You'll bring him to visit me and Blackberry sometimes.'

Inside the carrier, the glossy black rabbit was licking Arrow's ears, while the magic bunny's eyes were closed in contentment.

Dawn laughed. 'OK. Deal!'

Emma reached into the car, unfastened the carrier and lifted out Arrow. 'You'd better put him in your bag before your mum and dad see him. They're just coming out of the school,' she said, glancing over Dawn's shoulder.

'Oh, right. Thanks.' Dawn opened her bag. 'Quickly, Arrow!' Her fluffy white friend gave a mighty leap out of Emma's arms and dived straight inside.

Emma grinned, impressed. 'That was some jump! Anyone would think Arrow understood what you said!'

Dawn smiled back. *If only you knew*, she thought.

'See you in class on Monday!'

Emma called.

'See you! And thanks again.' Dawn
tried not to limp as she walked away.

Arrow leaned up out of her bag, so that
she could slip the golden chain round his
neck. 'Thank you for rescuing me and
returning my key! You are a very good
friend, Dawn.'

'I just couldn't bear the thought of
losing you. Oh!' Dawn gritted her teeth
and stumbled as pain zinged up her leg.
Her ankle was throbbing horribly.

Arrow's furry brow crinkled in
concern. 'You are hurt! I will help you.'

Dawn felt a warm prickling sensation
down her spine as Arrow's key started
pulsing with light. Arrow twitched his
little pink nose and a cloud of crystal dust
appeared, shimmering with a thousand

tiny rainbows. To Dawn's amazement, the magical dust swirled round her sore ankle for a few seconds, before seeming to sink into it. Her ankle turned icy cold before suddenly feeling fine — not even a twinge.

'Wow! Thanks, Arrow. I'm fine now. Come on. Let's go and find Mum and Dad and get you home!'

Chapter
EIGHT

Later that night, Arrow sat on Dawn's
bedroom window sill as they both looked
out at the starry sky. The moon was a
silver sickle overhead, spreading pale light
on the street below.

It had been a long exciting day. Dawn
bit back a yawn as she wondered if the
same moon shone down on Moonglow
Meadow.

Suddenly, Dawn felt Arrow stiffen
beside her. 'Look there!' Arrow pointed
with a front paw as a group of black
shapes crossed a pool of streetlight on the
opposite side of the road. 'Dark rabbits!
My enemies are close,' he said in
a panicky voice.

Dawn quickly snatched him up and
drew the curtains closed with her free

hand. She could feel him trembling.
'I don't think they saw you. And you're safe in here with me.'

Arrow leaned forward to peep out of a tiny crack in the curtains. 'The dark rabbits are moving away,' he said with relief.

Dawn hugged Arrow protectively until he calmed down. She put him on her bed.

Almost at once, the magic key began flashing more brightly than Dawn had ever seen it.

'Moonglow Meadow will soon be in need of more magic!' Arrow exclaimed.

Dawn gasped. 'Do you have to leave right now?' she asked anxiously.

'No. Not until the key glows constantly. But then I may have to leave at once without saying goodbye.'

Dawn bit back a surge of dismay. 'Will
. . . will you be coming back to live with
me again?'

Arrow looked up at her with gentle
soft brown eyes. 'I am afraid that is not
possible. Once I leave here, the magic trail
to this place is closed forever. I am sorry.
I hope you understand, Dawn.'

Dawn nodded sadly. She tried not to
think about Arrow leaving, especially after
almost losing him once already today. She
decided to enjoy every single moment of
the time they had left together.

The following afternoon, Dawn and
Arrow were sitting on the grass in a quiet
corner of the grounds that surrounded
Redford Mansions. Dawn munched on
some chocolate Easter egg as she watched

him investigating a patch of weeds. After she finished the egg, she squeezed the shiny wrapper into a tight ball.

'Hey, Arrow! Fancy learning to play fetch?' She rolled the ball towards him.

Arrow's ears swivelled. He looked up and then hopped forward and grasped the ball in his mouth.

'That's it,' Dawn encouraged. 'Bring it to me and I'll throw for you again.'

Arrow soon got the idea. They played fetch for a while until, at last, he flopped down, panting. 'That was fun!'

Dawn picked him up. 'Let's go inside and you can have a nap.'

The phone rang in the hall as they came in.

'I bet that's Aunt Jenny!' Dawn exclaimed eagerly as she answered it. 'Hi, Aunt Jen! Oh –' she paused in surprise as she realized who it was – 'Emma?'

'Hi, Dawn. I wondered if you and Arrow would like to come to my house for tea tomorrow? Mum says it's OK.'

'Um . . . I guess I could,' Dawn said, feeling unsure. She still wasn't quite used to this new friendly Emma.

'You don't have to, if you don't want to,' Emma said quietly.

Dawn made up her mind. 'I'd love to!'

'Great! This is where I live . . .'

*

'I'm glad that you're starting to make some new friends, love,' Mr Kenton said as he dropped Dawn and Arrow off at Emma's.

'Me too,' Dawn said.

The house was at the end of a row. There were pots of bright flowers on either side of a cheerful red front door. Dawn rang the bell. After a little while, when no one had appeared, she rang it again.

'I don't think anyone's in. I knew it! This is another of Emma's daft jokes!' she sighed. 'I bet she's been waiting all this time to pay me back for covering her in those sticky streamers in the cloakroom!'

A slight breeze stirred Arrow's fluffy white fur. He seemed disappointed. 'I was looking forward to seeing Blackberry again. He is a fine rabbit.'

'That's it. We're leaving!' Dawn was
turning away when the door opened.

'Sorry! I only just heard the bell,'
Emma said brightly. 'We were all in the
garden. Come in.'

Dawn calmed down as she followed
Emma into the house. She'd been totally
wrong about her this time.

Emma's mum greeted Dawn with a
warm smile. Delicious cooking smells
wafted out of the kitchen behind her.
'Hello, Dawn. This must be the little lost
white bunny you've adopted.'

'Hi, Mrs Packard,' Dawn said politely.
'Yes. He's called Arrow.'

'Why don't you show Dawn and
Arrow where Blackberry lives, Emma?
I'll call you when tea's ready.'

Emma led the way outside to a garden
shed and opened the door. 'Ta dah!'

'Wow! This is bunny heaven!' Dawn
said, admiring the smart hutch, neat
shelves and sturdy bunny run that was
scattered with toys. There were clean
dishes, packets of rabbit food and bags
of straw on shelves. The shed smelled of
sweet hay.

Arrow's pink nose was twitching in approval. 'This is a good place.'

'I'd forgotten how sweet Arrow is. Can I hold him please?' Emma asked.

Arrow didn't seem to mind so Dawn handed him over.

'Hi, Arrow,' Emma crooned, stroking him gently. 'Hasn't he got unusual eyes? They're like treacle toffee speckled with rainbow dust.'

'Arrow's one of a kind,' Dawn agreed.

'You can cuddle Blackberry, if you like.' Emma opened the hutch door, so Dawn could lift him out. 'I brushed him for ages so his coat is all shiny,' she said proudly.

At Emma's suggestion, they put the bunnies into the run. After some friendly nose twitching and fur snuffling, Arrow and Blackberry began rooting through

the straw and chewing toys.

'Look at that. Instant best friends!'
Emma grinned, her eyes sparkling. 'I love
animals.' She began talking about all the
pets she'd had. '. . . and a gerbil and two
rats. And I used to have a cute Yorkshire
terrier called Maisie. How about you?'

Dawn chewed at her lip. 'I've . . . I've
got a dog called Tansy. But she doesn't
live with me any more.' To her surprise,
once she started, it was easy to tell Emma

everything. When she'd finished she was biting back tears.

Emma listened in silence until Dawn had finished. 'Oh, poor you. That's so awful,' she sympathized. 'I'd hate it if I had to re-home Blackberry.' A look of determination came over her face. 'Your flat's in Redford Mansions, is it? There might be something we can do about Tansy. Leave it to me.'

Chapter
NINE

'It was fun at Emma's house today, wasn't it?' Dawn said to Arrow. After a delicious tea of sandwiches, cheese scones and Mrs Packard's amazing lemon cake, Emma's dad had driven them back to Redford Mansions.

'I had a good time too,' Arrow said as the lift door pinged open at their floor. 'It was nice of her to say she'd try to do something about Tansy, but I don't think anybody can.'

Arrow looked up at her. 'Emma seems to be a person who is true to her word.'

Dawn stroked the tiny rabbit fondly. 'Well, I do appreciate her wanting to help,' she agreed.

Dawn walked into the flat and found her mum in the hall. She had her coat on and looked worried. 'Mum? Is something wrong?'

Mrs Kenton nodded. 'I'm afraid Aunt Jenny's just phoned. It's Tansy. She's escaped somehow and run off.'

Dawn gasped. 'Oh no!'

Mrs Kenton grabbed her coat. 'Come on! We're going straight over to help look for her!'

Dawn's heart was in her mouth as they drove across town. She sat in silence, cuddling Arrow.

Aunt Jenny was apologetic. 'I'm so sorry, Dawn. Tansy must have slipped out when my back was turned. We've searched everywhere but there's no sign of her. I'm just about to phone the vet . . .'

Dawn knew what that meant. She tried not to think about busy roads and other dangers. 'Where can she be? I don't where to look,' she whispered to Arrow.

'I will help you!' His magical key
glowed as he pointed a little white paw
at the ground. A fountain of crystal dust
whooshed out, revealing a trail of glowing
doggy footprints that led up the road and
disappeared round the corner. 'This way,
Dawn!'

'Yay!' Dawn cheered, hastily turning it
into a cough as her mum and Aunt Jenny
turned to look at her in surprise. 'I've got
a hunch about where Tansy went!'

Dawn ran after Arrow, who was streaking away, his white bobtail flashing. She raced along, following the trail of glowing doggy footprints. As she turned a corner, she glimpsed Arrow's tiny form passing some shops along the high street.

This was where she and mum had gone shopping. Somehow Tansy must have picked up Dawn's trail. Arrow was following the shining pawprints that seemed to be going in the direction of Redford Mansions.

Dawn felt renewed hope as she put a spurt on. She was only seconds behind Arrow as she raced into the flat's gardens.

'What's that on the bench?' Dawn narrowed her eyes. 'It's not . . . It can't be! Tansy?' she gasped.

'Yes, Dawn. She is safe.'

Something in Arrow's voice made
Dawn look at him.

His magic key was glowing constantly
like a miniature gold star. The moment
Dawn had been dreading was here.
A cloud of shimmering crystal dust
appeared, swirling around Arrow and
twinkling with rainbow sparkles.

Suddenly, Arrow appeared in his true
form. A tiny fluffy white bunny no
longer, but a majestic rabbit the size of
a large cat. His silky pure white fur was
flecked with silver and his large ears had
glittering silver tips.

'Arrow!' Dawn gasped. She had almost
forgotten how beautiful he was. 'Are you
leaving right now?'

Sadness flickered across his chocolate
brown eyes for a moment. 'I must.

Moonglow Meadow urgently needs more of the key's magic.'

Dawn's eyes stung with tears. She bit them back as she knew she must be brave and allow her friend to go. She bent down and threw her arms around the handsome white rabbit and laid her cheek against his silky fur.

'I'll never forget you,' she whispered brokenly.

'I will not forget you either.' Arrow
allowed her to hug him one last time and
then moved gently away. 'Farewell. And
always follow your dreams, Dawn,' he said
in a velvety voice.

There was a final flash of light, and
crystal dust rained down around Dawn,
tinkling softly as it hit the ground. Arrow
faded and was gone.

Dawn stood there, stunned by how
fast everything had happened. Her chest
ached with the effort of holding back
tears. Something lay on the grass. It was
a single rainbow crystal drop. Bending
down, she picked it up. The drop tingled
against her palm as it turned into a tiny
pure white pebble in the shape of a
bunny.

Dawn slipped it into her pocket. She

knew she would always keep it as a reminder of the magic bunny and the wonderful adventure they had shared.

As she straightened up, Tansy rushed over, whining and wagging her tail. Dawn picked her up. 'Hello, girl! You're safe with me now.'

'Dawn!'

Dawn turned round to see Emma running towards her. 'I've got some brilliant news! Is this Tansy?'

Dawn blinked in puzzlement. 'Emma? What news? When did you get here?'

'My dad works for the company that owns Redford Mansions. He's got special permission for you to have Tansy living with you! I couldn't wait to tell you, so I got Dad to give me a lift over here.'

'But that's fantastic!' Dawn didn't know

whether to laugh or cry. She knew that
Arrow would be watching with approval.

*Take care. Wherever you are. And look after
Moonglow Meadow,* she whispered under
her breath.

And then she smiled at her new best
friend, Emma. 'What I really need is
someone who'll help take Tansy for walks.
Any ideas?'

Emma smiled back. 'You bet!'

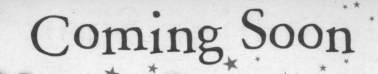

Coming Soon

Magic Bunny

Could you be this tiny bunny's special friend?

Magic Bunny

Holiday
Dreams

SUE BENTLEY

Coming Soon

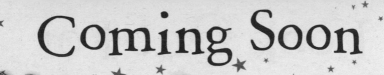

Magic Bunny

Could you be this tiny bunny's special friend?

Magic Bunny

Dancing Days

SUE BENTLEY

puffin.co.uk

Magic Ponies

A New Friend
9780141325934

A Special Wish
9780141325941

A Twinkle of Hooves
9780141325958

Showjumping Dreams
9780141325965

Seaside Summer
9780141325972

Riding Rescue
9780141325989

Winter Wonderland
9780141327723

Pony Camp
9780141327730

A Christmas Wish
9780141325996

puffin.co.uk

Magic Puppy

A New Beginning
9780141323503

Muddy Paws
9780141323510

Cloud Capers
9780141323527

Star of the Show
9780141323534

Party Dreams
9780141323794

A Forest Charm
9780141323800

Twirling Tails
9780141323817

School of Mischief
9780141323824

Snowy Wishes
9780141323831

Classroom Princess
9780141324791

Friendship Forever
9780141324784

Sparkling Skates
9780141324777

Sunshine Shimmers
9780141324760

Spellbound at School
9780141324753

The Perfect Secret
9780141324746

A little puppy
a sprinkling of magic,
a forever friend

puffin.co.uk

If you like
Magic Puppy,
you'll love

Magic
Kitten

A Summer Spell
9780141320144

Classroom Chaos
9780141320151

Star Dreams
9780141320168

Double Trouble
9780141320175

Moonlight Mischief
9780141321530

A Circus Wish
9780141321547

Sparkling Steps
9780141321554

A Glittering Gallop
9780141321561

Seaside Mystery
9780141321981

Firelight Friends
9780141321998

A Shimmering Splash
9780141322001

A Puzzle of Paws
9780141322018

A Christmas Surprise
9780141323237

Picture Perfect
9780141323480

A Splash of Forever
9780141323497

Magic Bunny

Win a Magic Bunny goody bag!

Strike, the leader of the bunnies of Moonglow Meadow,
has an urgent message for Arrow that will keep him safe from the
dark rabbits who are trying to capture the magic key.

Four words from the message can be found in the special carrots
that are hidden in this Magic Bunny book. Find the hidden
words and put them together to complete Strike's message.
Send it into us and each month we will put every correct message
in a draw and pick out one lucky winner who will
receive a special Magic Bunny prize.

Send your secret message, name and address on a postcard to:
Magic Bunny competition
Puffin Books
80 Strand
London WC2R 0RL

Hurry, Arrow needs your help!

Good luck!

It all started with a Scarecrow

Puffin is well over sixty years old.
Sounds ancient, doesn't it? But Puffin has never been
so lively. We're always on the lookout for the next big
idea, which is how it began all those years ago.

Penguin Books was a big idea from the mind of
a man called Allen Lane, who in 1935 invented
the quality paperback and changed the world.
**And from great Penguins, great Puffins grew,
changing the face of children's books forever.**

The first four Puffin Picture Books were hatched in 1940 and the
first Puffin story book featured a man with broomstick arms called
Worzel Gummidge. In 1967 Kaye Webb, Puffin Editor, started the
Puffin Club, promising to **'make children into readers'**.
She kept that promise and over 200,000 children became
devoted Puffineers through their quarterly instalments of
Puffin Post, which is now back for a new generation.

Many years from now, we hope you'll look back and
remember Puffin with a smile. **No matter what your age
or what you're into, there's a Puffin for everyone.**
The possibilities are endless, but one thing is for sure:
whether it's a picture book or a paperback, a sticker book
or a hardback, **if it's got that little Puffin
on it – it's bound to be good.**